Moon over the Mountain

Written by Keith Polette
Illustrated by Michael Kress-Russick

For Anthony, Avery, Perrin, and Danikan. ~ Keith

To Alan Russick, my father. ~ Michael

Text © 2009 by Keith Polette
Illustration © 2009 by Michael Kress–Russick

Polette, Keith.

  Moon Over the Mountain / written by Keith Polette; illustrated by Michael Kress–Russick;
–1 ed.–McHenry, IL: Raven Tree Press, 2009.

  p.;cm.

  SUMMARY: A retelling of an Asian folktale with a Southwest twist in which a
     discontented stonecutter is never satisfied with each wish that is
     granted him. Set in the desert Southwest.

English-Only Edition
ISBN 978-1-934960-07-3 hardcover

Bilingual Edition
ISBN 978-1-932748-85-7 hardcover
ISBN 978-1-932748-84-0 paperback

  Audience: pre–K to 3rd grade
  Title available in English-only or bilingual English-Spanish editions

  1. Fairy Tales & Folktales/Adaptation—Juvenile fiction. 2. Lifestyles/Country Life—
Juvenile fiction. I. Illust. Kress-Russick, Michael. II. Title.

LCCN: 2009926216

Printed in Taiwan
10 9 8 7 6 5 4 3 2 1
First Edition

Free activities for this book are available at www.raventreepress.com

Moon over the Mountain

Written by Keith Polette
Illustrated by Michael Kress-Russick

Raven Tree Press
A Division of Delta Systems Co., Inc.
www.raventreepress.com

Agipito was a poor stonecutter. Day after day, he cut out stones for large houses and churches. Cutting stones was hard work, so Agipito longed for an easier life. He thought his life could not be changed. He thought his life was set in stone.

4

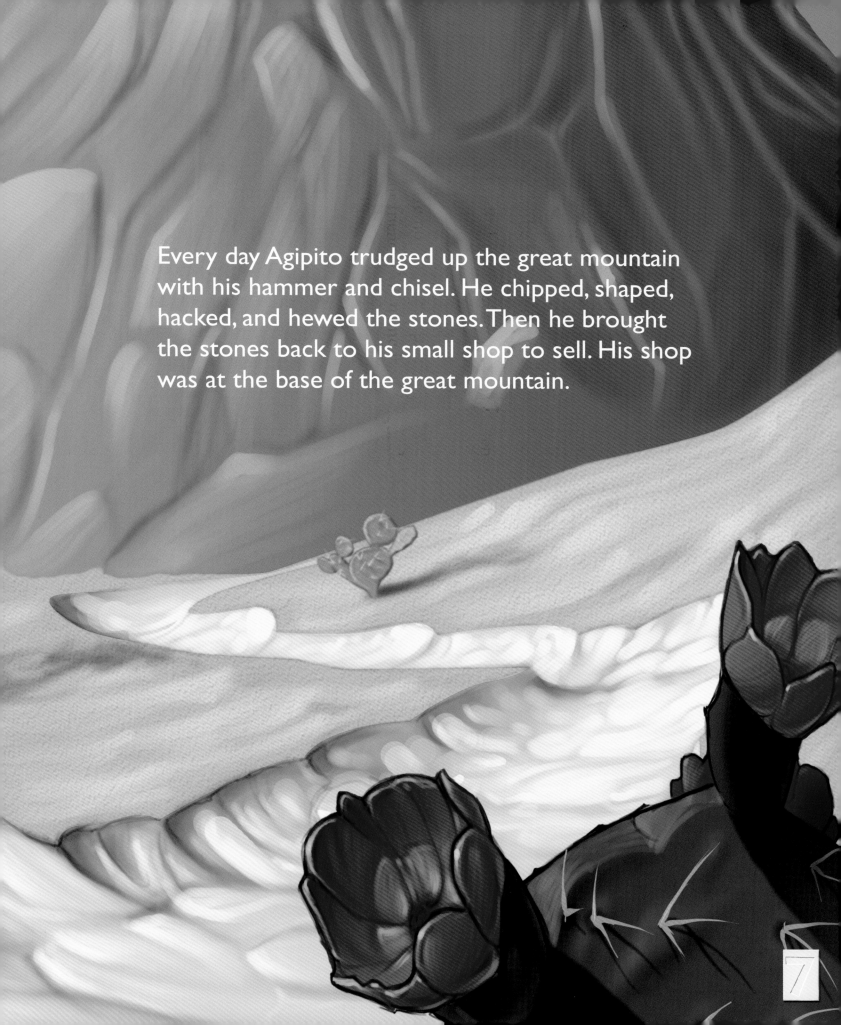

Every day Agipito trudged up the great mountain with his hammer and chisel. He chipped, shaped, hacked, and hewed the stones. Then he brought the stones back to his small shop to sell. His shop was at the base of the great mountain.

One hot afternoon, Agipito was dragging a sled of stones to his shop. As he wiped his face, he spotted the carriage of a rich merchant. Inside the carriage, the rich merchant was dressed in fine silk. Gold rings sparkled on his hands. The rich merchant ate sweet fruit that Agipito had never seen or tasted.

"Oh, how I wish I was a rich merchant!" Agipito said.

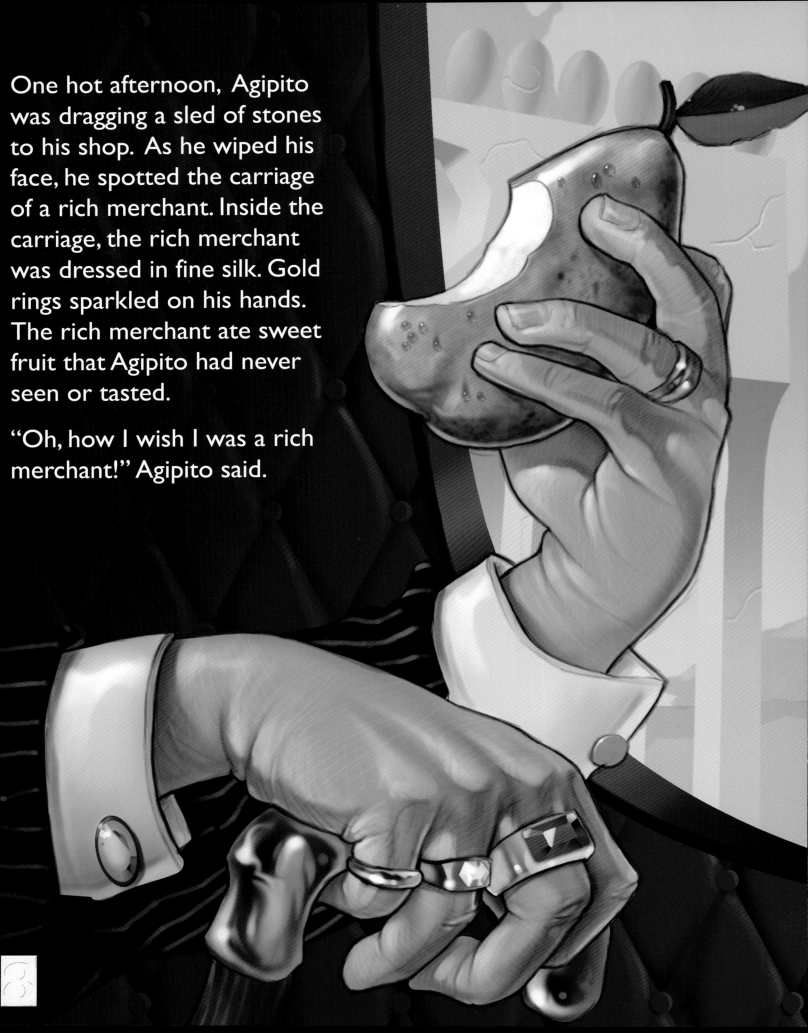

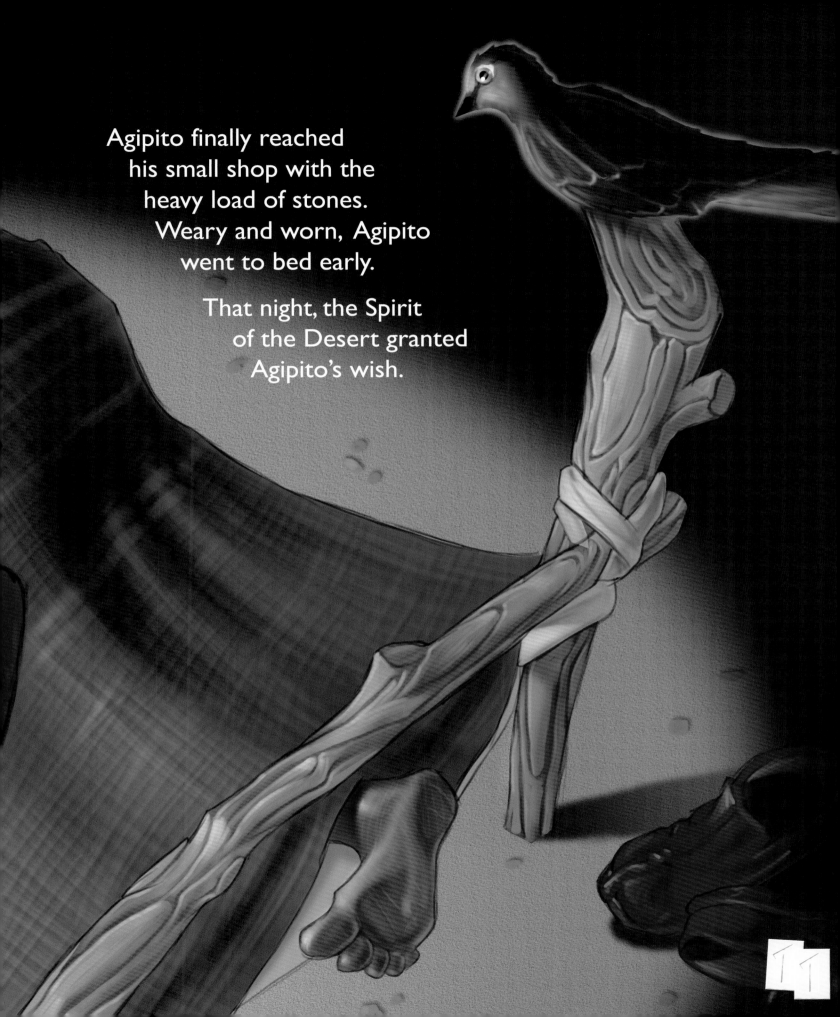

Agipito finally reached
his small shop with the
heavy load of stones.
Weary and worn, Agipito
went to bed early.

That night, the Spirit
of the Desert granted
Agipito's wish.

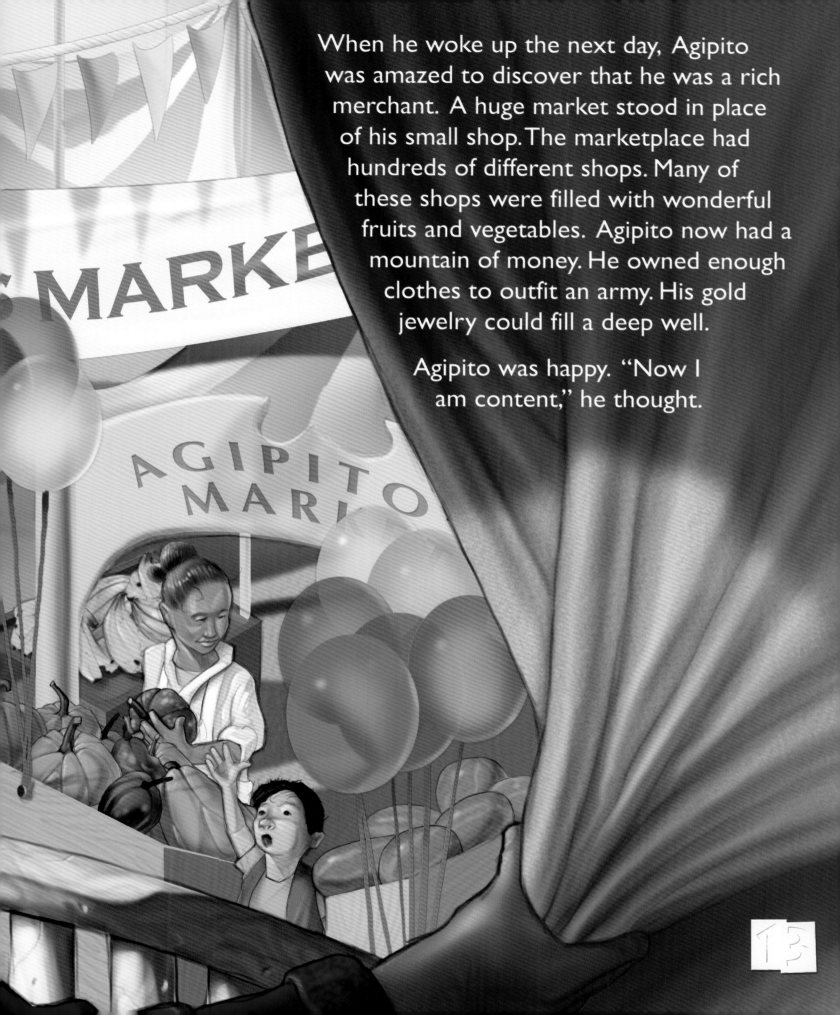

When he woke up the next day, Agipito was amazed to discover that he was a rich merchant. A huge market stood in place of his small shop. The marketplace had hundreds of different shops. Many of these shops were filled with wonderful fruits and vegetables. Agipito now had a mountain of money. He owned enough clothes to outfit an army. His gold jewelry could fill a deep well.

Agipito was happy. "Now I am content," he thought.

Agipito walked through his large market as the sun blazed in the blue sky. Beneath the scorching heat of the sun, the sweet fruits and crisp vegetables in his shops wilted. The hand-painted fabrics faded. People fainted from the heat.

Agipito saw the strength of the sun and said, "How I wish I was the sun!"

As Agipito slept that night, the Spirit of the Desert once again granted his wish.

When he awoke the next morning, Agipito was the sun. He laughed with fire and hurled handfuls of heat across the land. The ground cracked and the crops withered. The rivers and streams ran dry.

Agipito was content.

17

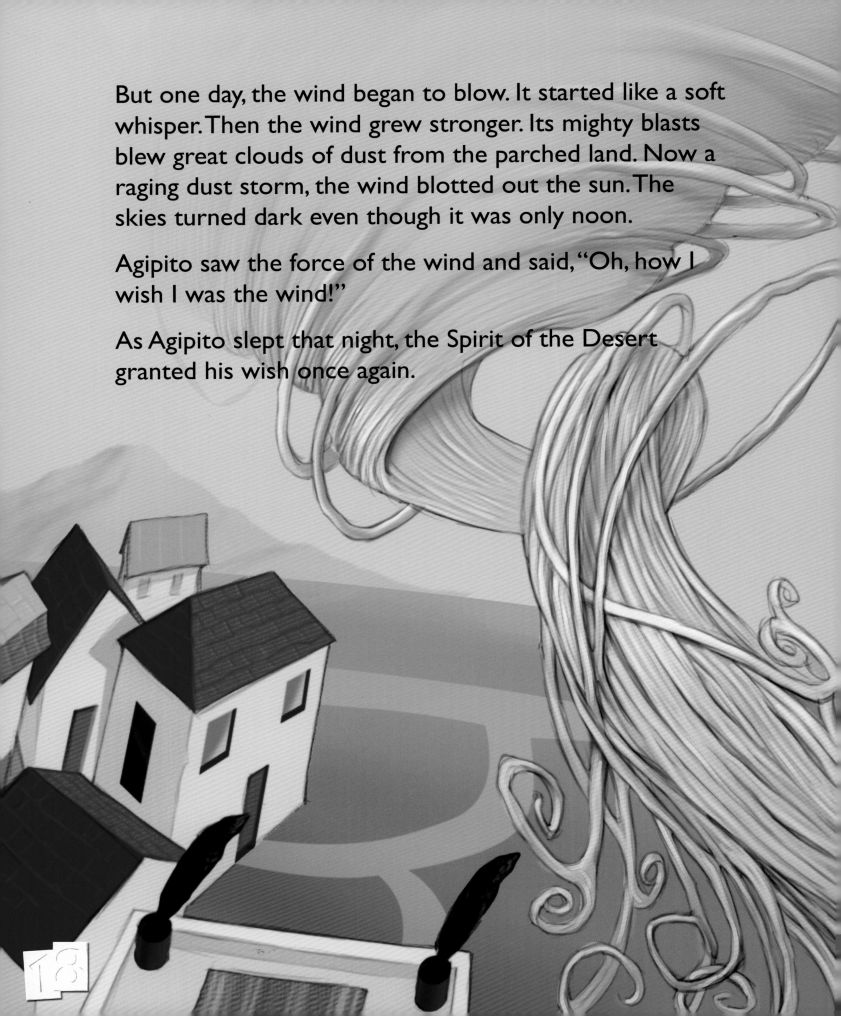

But one day, the wind began to blow. It started like a soft whisper. Then the wind grew stronger. Its mighty blasts blew great clouds of dust from the parched land. Now a raging dust storm, the wind blotted out the sun. The skies turned dark even though it was only noon.

Agipito saw the force of the wind and said, "Oh, how I wish I was the wind!"

As Agipito slept that night, the Spirit of the Desert granted his wish once again.

18

When the next day dawned, Agipito was the wind. He roared with delight and howled across the land. With his dust-filled gusts, Agipito sent carriages and wagons tumbling. He blew down the houses that were not made of stone.

Agipito was content—until he saw that the great mountain stood firm.

21

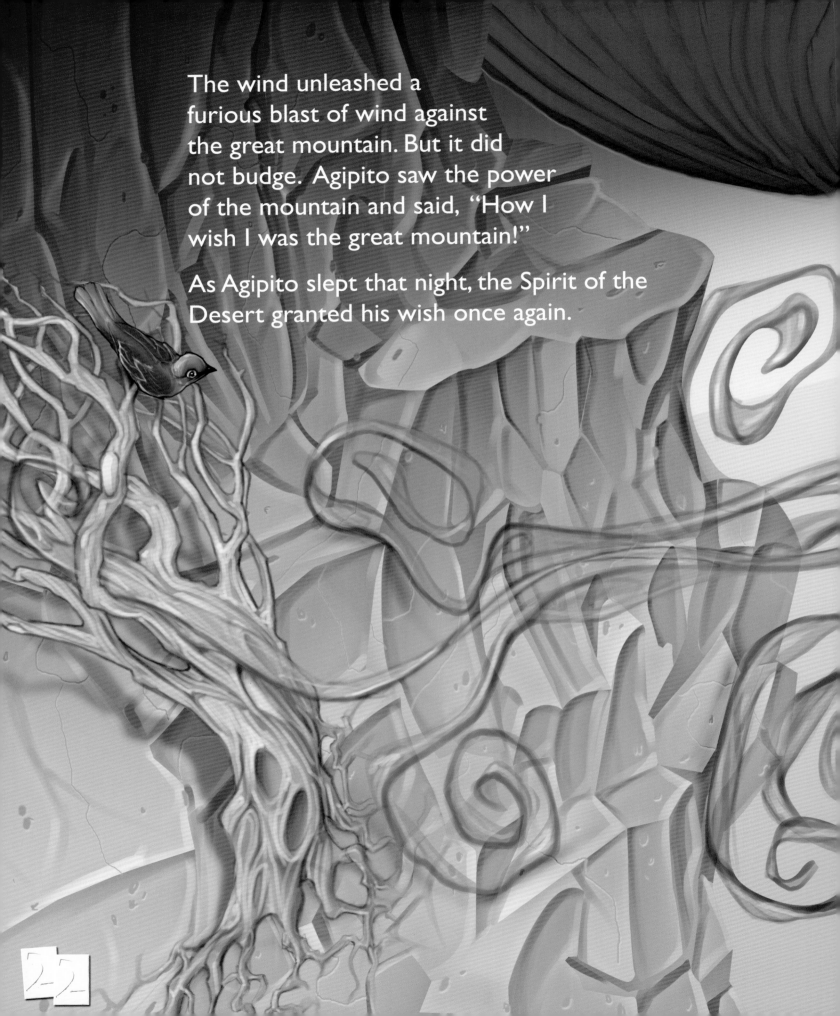

The wind unleashed a furious blast of wind against the great mountain. But it did not budge. Agipito saw the power of the mountain and said, "How I wish I was the great mountain!"

As Agipito slept that night, the Spirit of the Desert granted his wish once again.

The next day, Agipito was the great mountain. Agipito was now stronger than the rich merchant, more powerful than the sun, and mightier than the wind. He proudly towered over the land.

Agipito was very content.

Early one morning, Agipito woke up to the sounds of a hammer and chisel. A poor stonecutter was hacking and hewing the stones at the base of the great mountain.

Agipito shuddered and made one final wish. The Spirit of the Desert granted it.

26

When Agipito opened his eyes the next day, he was a coyote. His fur coat was silkier than the fancy clothes of the rich merchant. The eyes of the coyote flashed with the fire of the sun. His spirit was stronger than the great mountain. His life was no longer set in stone.

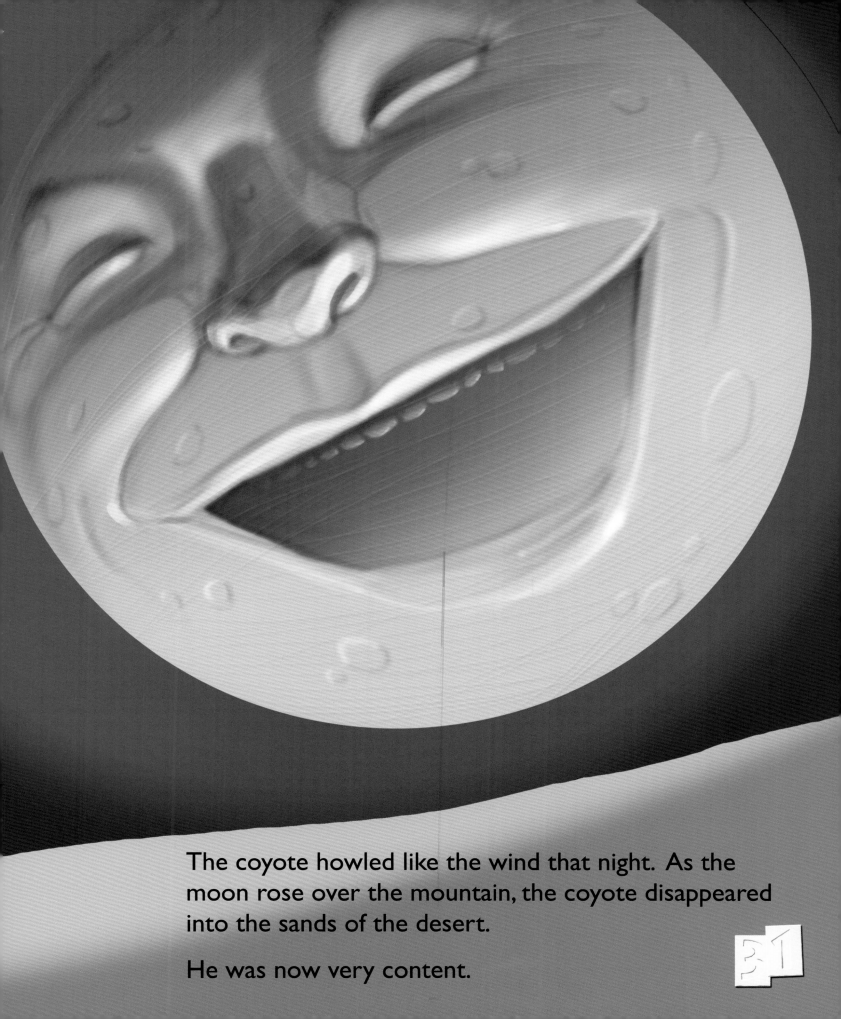

The coyote howled like the wind that night. As the moon rose over the mountain, the coyote disappeared into the sands of the desert.

He was now very content.